Library of Congress Cataloging-in-Publication Data
Emberley, Rebecca.
Mice on ice / by Rebecca Emberley and Ed Emberley. — 1st ed.
p. cm. — (I like to read)
Summary: Colorful mice go ice skating and are unexpectedly joined by a feline friend.
ISBN 978-0-8234-2576-1 (hardcover)
[1. Stories in rhyme. 2. Ice skating—Fiction. 3. Mice—Fiction. 4. Cats—Fiction.]
I. Emberley, Ed. II. Title.
PZ8.3.E517Mi 2012
782.42—dc23
[E]
2011038812

Mice
on
Ice

by Rebecca Emberley and Ed Emberley

Holiday House / New York

Mice walk on snow.

Mice skate on ice.

Mice on ice look nice.

Mice are skating.

Someone is waiting.

What is this?

What is that?

That is a cat.

That is a cat with a hat.

The cat with a hat skates
with mice on ice.

Nice!

I Like to Read® Books
You will like all of them!

Boy, Bird, and Dog by David McPhail
Dinosaurs Don't, Dinosaurs Do
     by Steve Björkman
Fish Had a Wish by Michael Garland
The Fly Flew In by David Catrow
I Will Try by Marilyn Janovitz
Late Nate in a Race by Emily Arnold McCully
The Lion and the Mice
     by Rebecca Emberley and Ed Emberley
Mice on Ice
     by Rebecca Emberley and Ed Emberley
Pig Has a Plan by Ethan Long
See Me Run by Paul Meisel
Sick Day by David McPhail

Visit holidayhouse.com to learn more
about I Like to Read® Books.